This book belongs to:

....

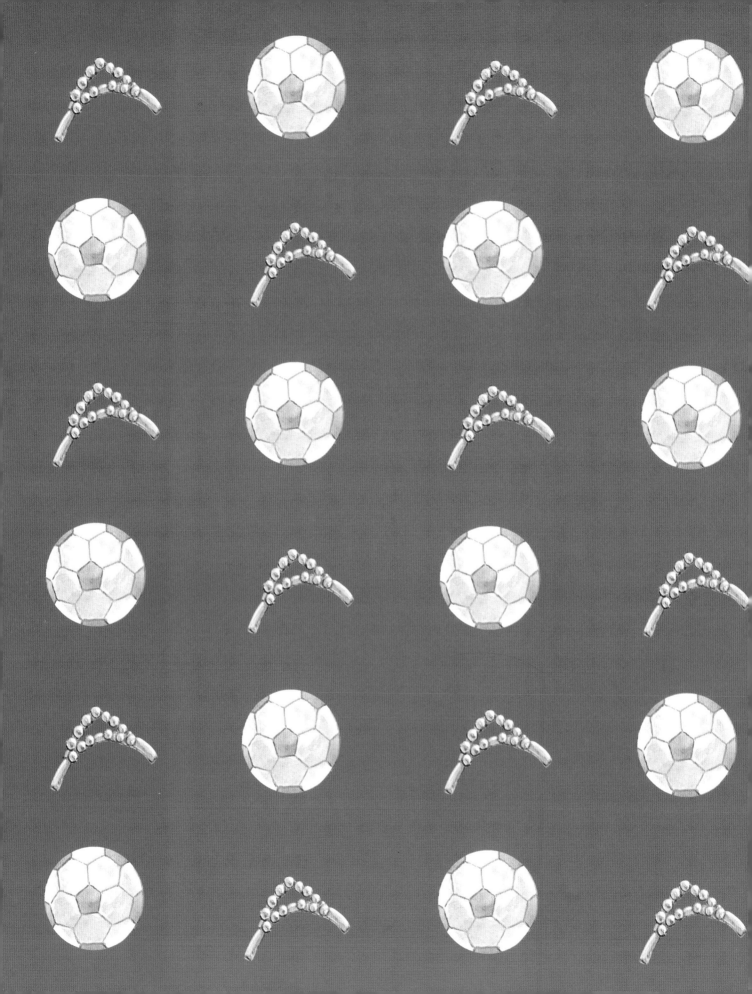

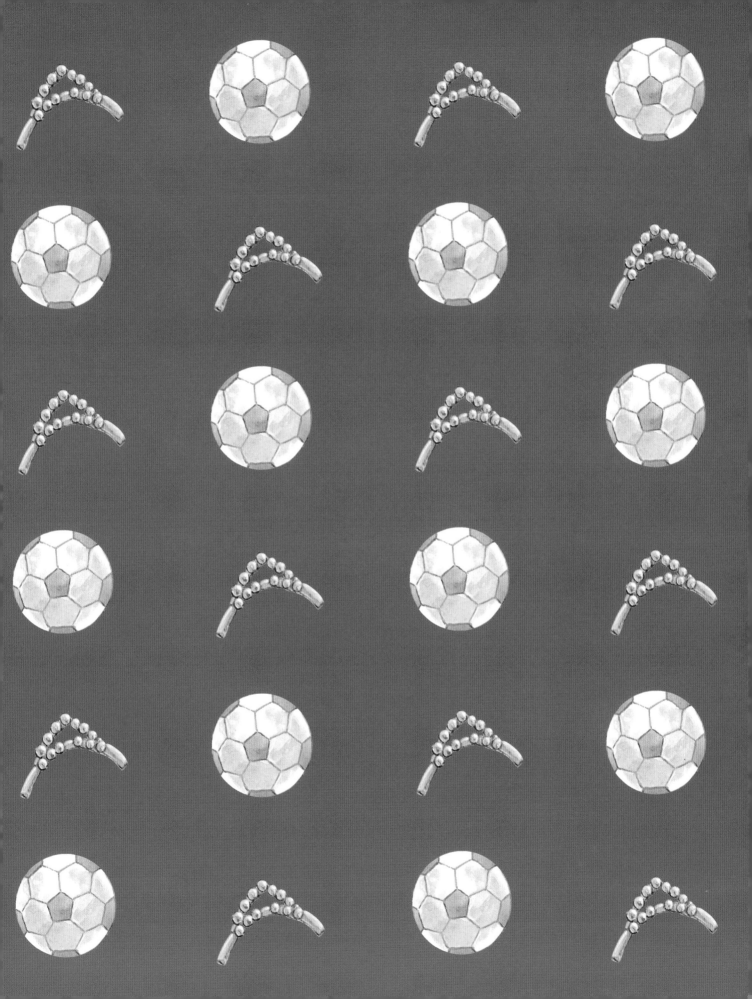

First published in Great Britain in 2003 by Brimax™,
an imprint of Octopus Publishing Group Ltd
2-4 Heron Quays, London E14 4JP

© Octopus Publishing Group Ltd 2003

A CIP catalogue record for this book is available
from the British Library.

ISBN 1 85854 450 5 (hardback)
ISBN 1 85854 704 0 (paperback)

Printed in China

Princess Fidgety Feet

Written by
Pat Posner

Illustrated by
Philip Norman

BRIMAX

Princess Bridget sighed deeply. She wished her mother would excuse her from the breakfast table.

She wanted to go and look through the telescope in the tower room.

Princess Bridget liked to watch children playing football in the school yard. The school was quite a long way from the castle, but looking through the telescope made everything seem much closer.

Princess Bridget secretly wanted
to play football, too. She thought
about it all the time, even when
she was doing princessly things.

Things like dancing
at the Royal Ball...

or waving to her
loyal subjects...

or greeting important visitors...

or watching opera with her
parents in the Royal Box.

Every Thursday afternoon, her friend Ryan, the palace paperboy, played football in the park. Princess Bridget always watched him through the telescope. When Ryan kicked the ball, Princess Bridget imagined kicking the ball. When he scored a goal, she scored a goal, too.

After delivering the palace newspapers, Ryan always hurried up to the tower room to play a quick game of football with Princess Bridget. It wasn't a princessly thing to do, so they had to be very quiet. They always played in the tower, as they thought no one else ever went up there.

Actually, the king often climbed up to the tower to watch them play, but Princess Bridget and Ryan never noticed!

Over her cornflakes, Princess Bridget was thinking about the game she and Ryan had played yesterday. First her left foot jerked, then her right foot jerked.

"Do keep still, Bridget," scolded the queen. "Princesses should not wriggle their feet at the table."

"But my feet want to move," Princess Bridget told her mother. "They want to run and jump and hop and leap."

"They should not want to run and jump and hop and leap *all* the time," said the queen with a sigh.

The king peered at his daughter over the top of his newspaper.

"I'll send for Miss Posy," he said. "Miss Posy will know what to do about fidgety feet."

The maid hid a giggle. Some of the royal staff secretly called Princess Bridget "Fidgety Feet".

Word of Miss Posy's arrival spread through the palace quickly. That afternoon, Ryan sprinted up to the tower room.

"Who's Miss Posy?" he panted.

Princess Bridget frowned. "I'm not sure," she said. "But Father told Mother that Miss Posy will teach me how to keep my head up, how to hold my shoulders back, and how to sit still..."

"Oh, Ryan, she'll teach me how to take short, neat steps. How can I play football if my feet take short, neat steps?" wailed Princess Bridget.

Princess Bridget sighed and looked through the telescope again. This time she was not watching children playing football in the school yard. Now, she was watching out for Miss Posy, who was expected to arrive by teatime.

At last, Miss Posy made her entrance.

"Lift your heads up high, stand up straight, keep your shoulders back, stick your chests out, and hold your tummies in!" Miss Posy ordered the royal guards.

"Bend from the knees, my man," she told a servant carrying a basket of logs to the fireplace in the Great Hall.

Next, Miss Posy marched into the kitchen, where the cook was preparing cucumber sandwiches.

"Those crusts don't look straight to me," she said.

At teatime, Miss Posy told Princess Bridget to sit up straight in her chair, keep her knees together, take dainty bites of her cucumber sandwich, and crook her little finger when she was drinking tea.

The next day, Miss Posy stuck pictures of footprints all along the Great Hall. Princess Bridget had to walk up and down, placing her feet inside the footprints. Then, to make matters worse, Miss Posy made Princess Bridget do it backwards – this time with three books on her head!

Poor Fidgety Feet, thought Ryan, who was peeking through the keyhole.

"Hurry up Thursday," Princess Bridget muttered to herself as she walked down the hall for the hundredth time." Thursday was Miss Posy's day off.

By the time Thursday came, Princess Bridget was behaving in a perfectly princessly way. She sat still at the table when she was reading.

She held her head high and kept her shoulders back when she walked.

"She isn't leaping and jumping and hopping. She's taking short, neat steps," the queen whispered to the king as they watched their daughter. "Miss Posy deserves her day off!"

"I wish I could play football," Princess Bridget told Ryan when he climbed up to the tower. "But I'm not sure I can. My feet have stopped wanting to run and jump and hop and leap. Horrible Miss Posy has made me prim and proper."

Ryan saw teardrops fall from Princess Bridget's eyes onto her rather large feet. He could not bear to see his friend so unhappy.

Later that morning, the king sent for Ryan and for two royal guards. He gave them a strange command. The guards told Princess Bridget they were taking her on a royal visit. But instead, they took her to the park.

"You're going to play on my team, Fidgety Feet," said Ryan. He had brought his spare football kit - boots, socks, a shirt, and a pair of shorts. Princess Bridget hid behind a big tree and changed into them.

A nervous but happy Princess Bridget stood in line with the rest of the team on the pitch. She kept her shoulders back, her chest out, and her tummy in. She didn't even wriggle her feet.

"I don't have fidgety feet any more," she whispered to Ryan. "I'm not sure if my feet want to kick the football."

But when the whistle blew, her feet *did* run and jump and hop and leap. They *wanted* to kick the football. They *did* kick the ball. First, her left foot kicked it into the goal. Then, her right foot kicked it into the goal! The crowd cheered when Princess Bridget's team won the game.

The king cheered as he
watched the game through the
telescope in the tower room.

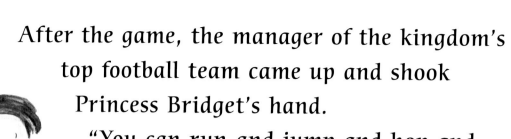

After the game, the manager of the kingdom's top football team came up and shook Princess Bridget's hand.

"You can run and jump and hop and leap and kick," he said. "But you also have discipline and control. All those things make a good footballer." Then he said, "I'd like you to play for our team. Our training sessions are every Thursday. The coach will see your parents tomorrow to arrange it."

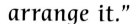

"It's a good thing Horrible Miss Posy has Thursdays off," said Princess Bridget to Ryan on the way back to the palace. "I know she taught me how to stop fidgeting, but I'm sure she'd think that playing football is a very unprincessly thing to do."

The next day, the king
summoned his daughter.

"Congratulations," he announced.
"You're to play on the top team.
Training is every Thursday. Now,
I'd like you to meet the coach."

Princess Bridget stared.
She could not believe her eyes!

"G-g-g-good morning,
Miss Posy," she spluttered.

The king laughed and said,
"I told you Miss Posy would sort things out."
"Ready for practice, Princess Bridget?" asked Miss Posy.
"I thought we'd do some drills in the Royal Gardens –
tower rooms really aren't the best place to play football!"

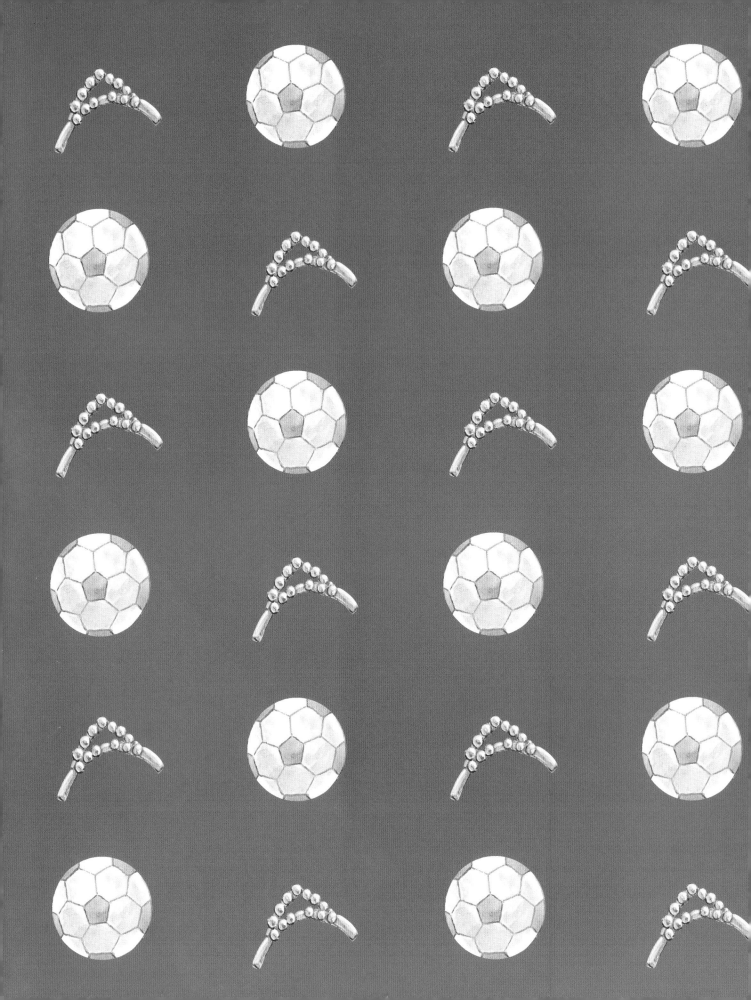

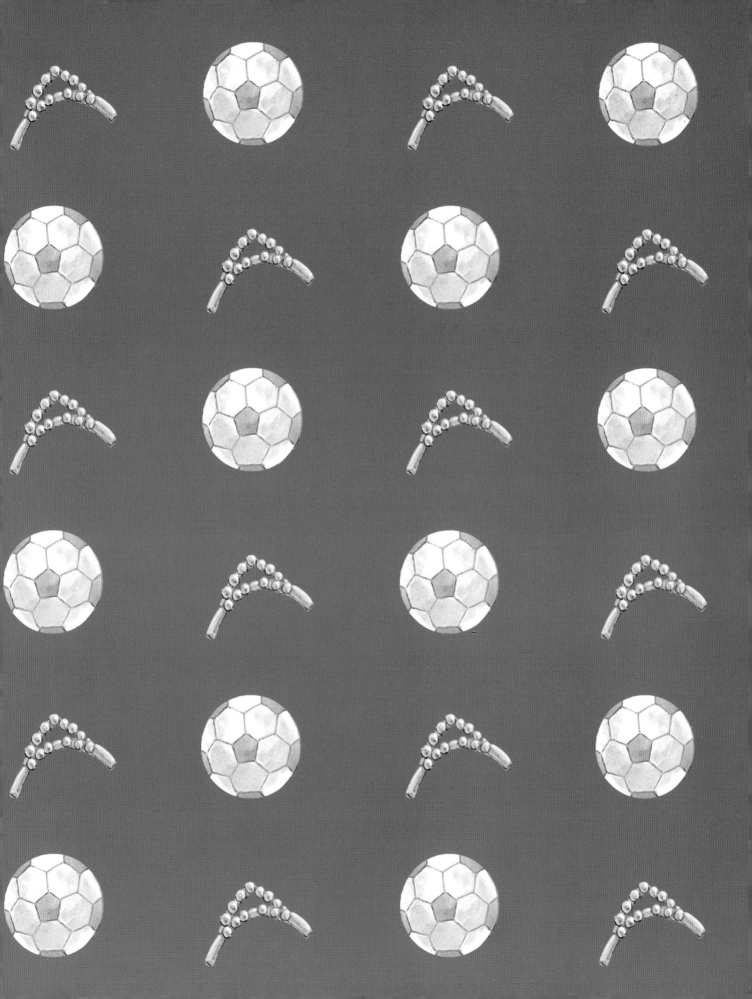